Henry James OM (15 April 1843 – 28 February 1916) was an American-British author regarded as a key transitional figure between literary realism and literary modernism, and is considered by many to be among the greatest novelists in the English language. He was the son of Henry James Sr. and the brother of renowned philosopher and psychologist William James and diarist Alice James.

He is best known for a number of novels dealing with the social and marital interplay between émigré Americans, English people, and continental Europeans. Examples of such novels include The Portrait of a Lady, The Ambassadors, and The Wings of the Dove. His later works were increasingly experimental. In describing the internal states of mind and social dynamics of his characters, James often made use of a style in which ambiguous or contradictory motives and impressions were overlaid or juxtaposed in the discussion of a character's psyche.(Source: Wikipedia)

Literary works:
Watch and Ward (1871)
Roderick Hudson (1875)
The American (1877)
The Europeans (1878)
Confidence (1879)
Washington Square (1880)
The Portrait of a Lady (1881)
The Bostonians (1886)
The Princess Casamassima (1886)
The Reverberator (1888)
The Tragic Muse (1890)
The Other House (1896)
The Spoils of Poynton (1897)
What Maisie Knew (1897)

PRINCE CLASSICS

THE
BELDONALD
HOLBEIN

HENRY JAMES

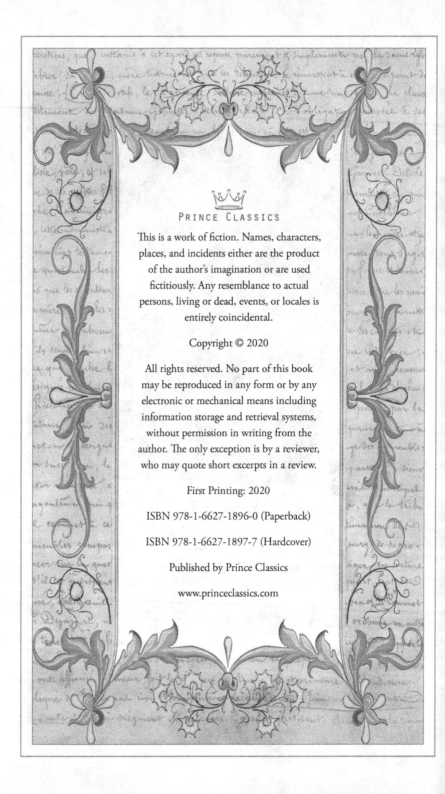

PRINCE CLASSICS

First Printing: 2020

ISBN 978-1-6627-1896-0 (Paperback)

ISBN 978-1-6627-1897-7 (Hardcover)

Published by Prince Classics

www.princeclassics.com

Contents

THE
BELDONALD
HOLBEIN

CHAPTER I

Mrs. Munden had not yet been to my studio on so good a pretext as when she first intimated that it would be quite open to me—should I only care, as she called it, to throw the handkerchief—to paint her beautiful sister-in-law. I needn't go here more than is essential into the question of Mrs. Munden, who would really, by the way, be a story in herself. She has a manner of her own of putting things, and some of those she has put to me—! Her implication was that Lady Beldonald hadn't only seen and admired certain examples of my work, but had literally been prepossessed in favour of the painter's "personality." Had I been struck with this sketch I might easily have imagined her ladyship was throwing me the handkerchief. "She hasn't done," my visitor said, "what she ought."

"Do you mean she has done what she oughtn't?"

"Nothing horrid—ah dear no." And something in Mrs. Munden's tone, with the way she appeared to muse a moment, even suggested to me that what she "oughtn't" was perhaps what Lady Beldonald had too much neglected. "She hasn't got on."

"What's the matter with her?"

"Well, to begin with, she's American."

"But I thought that was the way of ways to get on."

"It's one of them. But it's one of the ways of being awfully out of it too. There are so many!"

"So many Americans?" I asked.

"Yes, plenty of *them*," Mrs. Munden sighed. "So many ways, I mean, of being one."

"But if your sister-in-law's way is to be beautiful—?"

"Oh there are different ways of that too."

"And she hasn't taken the right way?"

"Well," my friend returned as if it were rather difficult to express, "she hasn't done with it—"

"I see," I laughed; "what she oughtn't!"

Mrs. Munden in a manner corrected me, but it *was* difficult to express. "My brother at all events was certainly selfish. Till he died she was almost never in London; they wintered, year after year, for what he supposed to be his health—which it didn't help, since he was so much too soon to meet his end—in the south of France and in the dullest holes he could pick out, and when they came back to England he always kept her in the country. I must say for her that she always behaved beautifully. Since his death she has been more in London, but on a stupidly unsuccessful footing. I don't think she quite understands. She hasn't what I should call a life. It may be of course that she doesn't want one. That's just what I can't exactly find out. I can't make out how much she knows."

"I can easily make out," I returned with hilarity, "how much *you* do!"

"Well, you're very horrid. Perhaps she's too old."

"Too old for what?" I persisted.

"For anything. Of course she's no longer even a little young; only preserved—oh but preserved, like bottled fruit, in syrup! I want to help her if only because she gets on my nerves, and I really think the way of it would be just the right thing of yours at the Academy and on the line."

"But suppose," I threw out, "she should give on my nerves?"

"Oh she will. But isn't that all in the day's work, and don't great beauties always—?"

"*You* don't," I interrupted; but I at any rate saw Lady Beldonald later on—the day came when her kinswoman brought her, and then I saw how her life must have its centre in her own idea of her appearance. Nothing else about her mattered—one knew her all when one knew that. She's indeed in one particular, I think, sole of her kind—a person whom vanity has had the odd effect of keeping positively safe and sound. This passion is supposed surely, for the most part, to be a principle of perversion and of injury, leading astray those who listen to it and landing them sooner or later in this or that complication; but it has landed her ladyship nowhere whatever—it has kept her from the first moment of full consciousness, one feels, exactly in the same place. It has protected her from every danger, has made her absolutely proper and prim. If she's "preserved," as Mrs. Munden originally described her to me, it's her vanity that has beautifully done it—putting her years ago in a plate-glass case and closing up the receptacle against every breath of air. How shouldn't she be preserved when you might smash your knuckles on this transparency before you could crack it? And she is—oh amazingly! Preservation is scarce the word for the rare condition of her surface. She looks *naturally* new, as if she took out every night her large lovely varnished eyes and put them in water. The thing was to paint her, I perceived, in the glass case—a most tempting attaching feat; render to the full the shining interposing plate and the general show-window effect.

It was agreed, though it wasn't quite arranged, that she should sit to me. If it wasn't quite arranged this was because, as I was made to understand from an early stage, the conditions from our start must be such as should exclude all elements of disturbance, such, in a word, as she herself should judge absolutely favourable. And it seemed that these conditions were easily imperilled. Suddenly, for instance, at a moment when I was expecting her to meet an appointment—the first—that I had proposed, I received a hurried visit from Mrs. Munden, who came on her behalf to let me know that the season happened just not to be propitious and that our friend couldn't be quite sure, to the hour, when it would again become so. She felt nothing would make it so but a total absence of worry.

"Oh a 'total absence,'" I said, "is a large order! We live in a worrying world."

"Yes; and she feels exactly that—more than you'd think. It's in fact just why she mustn't have, as she has now, a particular distress on at the very moment. She wants of course to look her best, and such things tell on her appearance."

I shook my head. "Nothing tells on her appearance. Nothing reaches it in any way; nothing gets *at* it. However, I can understand her anxiety. But what's her particular distress?"

"Why the illness of Miss Dadd."

"And who in the world's Miss Dadd?"

"Her most intimate friend and constant companion—the lady who was with us here that first day."

"Oh the little round black woman who gurgled with admiration?"

"None other. But she was taken ill last week, and it may very well be that she'll gurgle no more. She was very bad yesterday and is no better to-day, and Nina's much upset. If anything happens to Miss Dadd she'll have to get another, and, though she has had two or three before, that won't be so easy."

"Two or three Miss Dadds? is it possible? And still wanting another!" I recalled the poor lady completely now. "No; I shouldn't indeed think it would be easy to get another. But why is a succession of them necessary to Lady Beldonald's existence?"

"Can't you guess?" Mrs. Munden looked deep, yet impatient. "They help."

"Help what? Help whom?"

"Why every one. You and me for instance. To do what? Why to think Nina beautiful. She has them for that purpose; they serve as foils, as accents serve on syllables, as terms of comparison. They make her 'stand out.' It's an effect of contrast that must be familiar to you artists; it's what a woman does when she puts a band of black velvet under a pearl ornament that may, require, as she thinks, a little showing off."

I wondered. "Do you mean she always has them black?"

"Dear no; I've seen them blue, green, yellow. They may be what they like, so long as they're always one other thing."

"Hideous?"

Mrs. Munden made a mouth for it. "Hideous is too much to say; she doesn't really require them as bad as that. But consistently, cheerfully, loyally plain. It's really a most happy relation. She loves them for it."

"And for what do they love *her*?"

"Why just for the amiability that they produce in her. Then also for their 'home.' It's a career for them."

"I see. But if that's the case," I asked, "why are they so difficult to find?"

"Oh they must be safe; it's all in that: her being able to depend on them to keep to the terms of the bargain and never have moments of rising—as even the ugliest woman will now and then (say when she's in love)—superior to themselves."

I turned it over. "Then if they can't inspire passions the poor things mayn't even at least feel them?"

"She distinctly deprecates it. That's why such a man as you may be after all a complication."

I continued to brood. "You're very sure Miss Dadd's ailment isn't an affection that, being smothered, has struck in?" My joke, however, wasn't well timed, for I afterwards learned that the unfortunate lady's state had been, even while I spoke, such as to forbid all hope. The worst symptoms had appeared; she was destined not to recover; and a week later I heard from Mrs. Munden that she would in fact "gurgle" no more.

CHAPTER II

All this had been for Lady Beldonald an agitation so great that access to her apartment was denied for a time even to her sister-in-law. It was much more out of the question of course that she should unveil her face to a person of my special business with it; so that the question of the portrait was by common consent left to depend on that of the installation of a successor to her late companion. Such a successor, I gathered from Mrs. Munden, widowed childless and lonely, as well as inapt for the minor offices, she had absolutely to have; a more or less humble *alter ago* to deal with the servants, keep the accounts, make the tea and watch the window-blinds. Nothing seemed more natural than that she should marry again, and obviously that might come; yet the predecessors of Miss Dadd had been contemporaneous with a first husband, so that others formed in her image might be contemporaneous with a second. I was much occupied in those months at any rate, and these questions and their ramifications losing themselves for a while to my view, I was only brought back to them by Mrs. Munden's arrival one day with the news that we were all right again—her sister-in-law was once more "suited." A certain Mrs. Brash, an American relative whom she hadn't seen for years, but with whom she had continued to communicate, was to come out to her immediately; and this person, it appeared, could be quite trusted to meet the conditions. She was ugly—ugly enough, without abuse of it, and was unlimitedly good. The position offered her by Lady Beldonald was moreover exactly what she needed; widowed also, after many troubles and reverses, with her fortune of the smallest, and her various children either buried or placed about, she had never had time or means to visit England, and would really be grateful in her declining years for the new experience and the pleasant light work involved in her cousin's hospitality. They had been much together early in life and Lady Beldonald was immensely fond of her—would in fact have tried to get hold of her before hadn't Mrs. Brash been always in bondage to family duties, to the variety of her tribulations. I daresay I laughed at my friend's use of the term "position"—the position, one might call it, of a candlestick or a sign-post, and I daresay I must have asked if the special service the poor lady was to render had been made clear to her. Mrs. Munden left me in any case with the rather droll image of her faring forth across the sea quite consciously and resignedly to perform it.

The point of the communication had however been that my sitter was again looking up and would doubtless, on the arrival and due initiation of Mrs. Brash, be in form really to wait on me. The situation must further, to my knowledge, have developed happily, for I arranged with Mrs. Munden that our friend, now all ready to begin, but wanting first just to see the things I had most recently done, should come once more, as a final preliminary, to my studio. A good foreign friend of mine, a French painter, Paul Outreau, was at the moment in London, and I had proposed, as he was much interested in types, to get together for his amusement a small afternoon party. Every one came, my big room was full, there was music and a modest spread; and I've not forgotten the light of admiration in Outreau's expressive face as at the end of half an hour he came up to me in his enthusiasm. "*Bonté divine, mon cher—que cette vieille est donc belle!*"

I had tried to collect all the beauty I could, and also all the youth, so that for a moment I was at a loss. I had talked to many people and provided for the music, and there were figures in the crowd that were still lost to me. "What old woman do you mean?"

"I don't know her name—she was over by the door a moment ago. I asked somebody and was told, I think, that she's American."

I looked about and saw one of my guests attach a pair of fine eyes to Outreau very much as if she knew he must be talking of her. "Oh Lady Beldonald! Yes, she's handsome; but the great point about her is that she has been 'put up' to keep, and that she wouldn't be flattered if she knew you spoke of her as old. A box of sardines is 'old' only after it has been opened, Lady Beldonald never has yet been—but I'm going to do it." I joked, but I was somewhat disappointed. It was a type that, with his unerring sense for the *banal*, I shouldn't have expected Outreau to pick out.

15

"You're going to paint her? But, my dear man, she is painted—and as neither you nor I can do it. *Où est-elle donc?* He had lost her, and I saw I had made a mistake. She's the greatest of all the great Holbeins."

I was relieved. "Ah then not Lady Beldonald! But do I possess a Holbein of *any* price unawares?"

"There she is—there she is! Dear, dear, dear, what a head!" And I saw whom he meant—and what: a small old lady in a black dress and a black bonnet, both relieved with a little white, who had evidently just changed, her place to reach a corner from which more of the room and of the scene was presented to her. She appeared unnoticed and unknown, and I immediately recognised that some other guest must have brought her and, for want of opportunity, had as yet to call my attention to her. But two things, simultaneously with this and with each other, struck me with force; one of them the truth of Outreau's description of her, the other the fact that the person bringing her could only have been Lady Beldonald. She *was* a Holbein—of the first water; yet she was also Mrs. Brash, the imported "foil," the indispensable "accent," the successor to the dreary Miss Dadd! By the time I had put these things together—Outreau's "American" having helped me—I was in just such full possession of her face as I had found myself, on the other first occasion, of that of her patroness. Only with so different a consequence. I couldn't look at her enough, and I stared and stared till I became aware she might have fancied me challenging her as a person unpresented. "All the same," Outreau went on, equally held, "*c'est une tête à faire.* If I were only staying long enough for a crack at her! But I tell you what"—and he seized my arm—"bring her over!"

"Over?"

"To Paris. She'd have a *succès fou.*"

"Ah thanks, my dear fellow," I was now quite in a position to say; "she's the handsomest thing in London, and"—for what I might do with her was already before me with intensity—"I propose to keep her to myself." It was before me with intensity, in the light of Mrs. Brash's distant perfection of a little white old face, in which every wrinkle was the touch of a master; but something else, I suddenly felt, was not less so, for Lady Beldonald, in the other quarter, and though she couldn't have made out the subject of our notice, continued to fix us, and her eyes had the challenge of those of the woman of consequence who has missed something. A moment later I was close to her, apologising first for not having been more on the spot at her arrival, but saying in the next breath uncontrollably: "Why my dear lady, it's a Holbein!"

"A Holbein? What?"

"Why the wonderful sharp old face so extraordinarily, consummately drawn—in the frame of black velvet. That of Mrs. Brash, I mean—isn't it her name?—your companion."

This was the beginning of a most odd matter—the essence of my anecdote; and I think the very first note of the oddity must have sounded for me in the tone in which her ladyship spoke after giving me a silent look. It seemed to come to me out of a distance immeasurably removed from Holbein. "Mrs. Brash isn't my 'companion' in the sense you appear to mean. She's my rather near relation and a very dear old friend. I love her—and you must know her."

"Know her? Rather! Why to see her is to want on the spot to 'go' for her. She also must sit for me,"

"*She*? Louisa Brash?" If Lady Beldonald had the theory that her beauty directly showed it when things weren't well with her, this impression, which the fixed sweetness of her serenity had hitherto struck me by no means as justifying, gave me now my first glimpse of its grounds. It was as if I had never before seen her face invaded by anything I should have called an expression. This expression moreover was of the faintest—was like the effect produced on a surface by an agitation both deep within and as yet much confused. "Have you told her so?" she then quickly asked, as if to soften the sound of her surprise.

"Dear no, I've but just noticed her—Outreau, a moment ago put me on her. But we're both so taken, and he also wants—"

17

"To *paint* her?" Lady Beldonald uncontrollably murmured.

"Don't be afraid we shall fight for her," I returned with a laugh for this tone. Mrs. Brash was still where I could see her without appearing to stare, and she mightn't have seen I was looking at her, though her protectress, I'm afraid, could scarce have failed of that certainty. "We must each take our turn, and at any rate she's a wonderful thing, so that if you'll let her go to Paris Outreau promises her there—"

"*There?*" my companion gasped.

"A career bigger still than among us, as he considers we haven't half their eye. He guarantees her *a succès fou.*"

She couldn't get over it. "Louisa Brash? In Paris?"

"They do see," I went on, "more than we and they live extraordinarily, don't you know, in that. But she'll do something here too."

"And what will she do?"

If frankly now I couldn't help giving Mrs. Brash a longer look, so after it I could as little resist sounding my converser. "You'll see. Only give her time."

She said nothing during the moment in which she met my eyes; but then: "Time, it seems to me, is exactly what you and your friend want. If you haven't talked with her—"

"We haven't seen her? Oh we see bang off—with a click like a steel spring. It's our trade, it's our life, and we should be donkeys if we made mistakes. That's the way I saw you yourself, my lady, if I may say so; that's the way, with a long pin straight through your body, I've got you. And just so I've got *her!*"

All this, for reasons, had brought my guest to her feet; but her eyes had while we talked never once followed the direction of mine. "You call her a Holbein?"

18

"Outreau did, and I of course immediately recognised it. Don't you? She brings the old boy to life! It's just as I should call you a Titian. You bring *him* to life."

She couldn't be said to relax, because she couldn't be said to have hardened; but something at any rate on this took place in her—something indeed quite disconnected from what I would have called her. "Don't you understand that she has always been supposed—?" It had the ring of impatience; nevertheless it stopped short on a scruple.

I knew what it was, however, well enough to say it for her if she preferred. "To be nothing whatever to look at? To be unfortunately plain— or even if you like repulsively ugly? Oh yes, I understand it perfectly, just as I understand—I have to as a part of my trade—many other forms of stupidity. It's nothing new to one that ninety-nine people out of a hundred have no eyes, no sense, no taste. There are whole communities impenetrably sealed. I don't say your friend's a person to make the men turn round in Regent Street. But it adds to the joy of the few who do see that they have it so much to themselves. Where in the world can she have lived? You must tell me all about that—or rather, if she'll be so good, *she* must."

"You mean then to speak to her—?"

I wondered as she pulled up again. "Of her beauty?"

"Her beauty!" cried Lady Beldonald so loud that two or three persons looked round.

"Ah with every precaution of respect!" I declared in a much lower tone. But her back was by this time turned to me, and in the movement, as it were, one of the strangest little dramas I've ever known was well launched.

CHAPTER III

It was a drama of small smothered intensely private things, and I knew of but one other person in the secret; yet that person and I found it exquisitely susceptible of notation, followed it with an interest the mutual communication of which did much for our enjoyment, and were present with emotion at its touching catastrophe. The small case—for so small a case—had made a great stride even before my little party separated, and in fact within the next ten minutes.

In that space of time two things had happened one of which was that I made the acquaintance of Mrs. Brash; and the other that Mrs. Munden reached me, cleaving the crowd, with one of her usual pieces of news. What she had to impart was that, on her having just before asked Nina if the conditions of our sitting had been arranged with me, Nina had replied, with something like perversity, that she didn't propose to arrange them, that the whole affair was "off" again and that she preferred not to be further beset for the present. The question for Mrs. Munden was naturally what had happened and whether I understood. Oh I understood perfectly, and what I at first most understood was that even when I had brought in the name of Mrs. Brash intelligence wasn't yet in Mrs. Munden. She was quite as surprised as Lady Beldonald had been on hearing of the esteem in which I held Mrs. Brash's appearance. She was stupefied at learning that I had just in my ardour proposed to its proprietress to sit to me. Only she came round promptly—which Lady Beldonald really never did. Mrs. Munden was in fact wonderful; for when I had given her quickly "Why she's a Holbein, you know, absolutely," she took it up, after a first fine vacancy, with an immediate abysmal "Oh *is* she?" that, as a piece of social gymnastics, did her the greatest honour; and she was in fact the first in London to spread the tidings. For a face—about it was magnificent. But she was also the first, I must add, to see what would really happen—though this she put before me only a week or two later. "It will kill her, my dear—that's what it will do!"

She meant neither more nor less than that it would kill Lady Beldonald if I were to paint Mrs. Brash; for at this lurid light had we arrived in so short a space of time. It was for me to decide whether my æsthetic need of giving life to my idea was such as to justify me in destroying it in a woman after all in most eyes so beautiful. The situation was indeed sufficiently queer; for it remained to be seen what I should positively gain by giving up Mrs. Brash. I appeared to have in any case lost Lady Beldonald, now too "upset"—it was always Mrs. Munden's word about her and, as I inferred, her own about herself—to meet me again on our previous footing. The only thing, I of course soon saw, was to temporise to drop the whole question for the present and yet so far as possible keep each of the pair in view. I may as well say at once that this plan and this process gave their principal interest to the next several months. Mrs. Brash had turned up, if I remember, early in the new year, and her little wonderful career was in our particular circle one of the features of the following season. It was at all events for myself the most attaching; it's not my fault if I am so put together as often to find more life in situations obscure and subject to interpretation than in the gross rattle of the foreground. And there were all sorts of things, things touching, amusing, mystifying—and above all such an instance as I had never yet met—in this funny little fortune of the useful American cousin. Mrs. Munden was promptly at one with me as to the rarity and, to a near and human view, the beauty and interest of the position. We had neither of us ever before seen that degree and that special sort of personal success come to a woman for the first time so late in life. I found it an example of poetic, of absolutely retributive justice; so that my desire grew great to work it, as we say, on those lines. I had seen it all from the original moment at my studio; the poor lady had never known an hour's appreciation—which moreover, in perfect good faith, she had never missed. The very first thing I did after inducing so unintentionally the resentful retreat of her protectress had been to go straight over to her and say almost without preliminaries that I should hold myself immeasurably obliged for a few patient sittings. What I thus came face to face with was, on the instant, her whole unenlightened past and the full, if foreshortened, revelation of what among us all was now unfailingly in store for her. To turn the handle and start that tune came to me on the spot as a temptation. Here was a poor lady who had waited for the approach of old age to find out what she was worth. Here was a benighted being to whom it was to be disclosed in her fifty-seventh year—I was to make that out—that she had something that might pass for a face. She looked much more than her age, and was fairly frightened—as if I had been trying on her some possibly heartless London trick—when she had taken in my appeal. That showed me in what an air she had lived and—as I should have been tempted to put it had I spoken out—among what children of darkness. Later on I did them more justice; saw more that her wonderful points must have been points largely the fruit of time, and even that possibly she might never in all her life have looked so well as at this particular moment. It might have been that if her hour had struck I just happened to be present at the striking. What had occurred, all the same, was at the worst a notable comedy.

The famous "irony of fate" takes many forms, but I had never yet seen it take quite this one. She had been "had over" on an understanding, and she wasn't playing fair. She had broken the law of her ugliness and had turned beautiful on the hands of her employer. More interesting even perhaps than a view of the conscious triumph that this might prepare for her, and of which, had I doubted of my own judgement, I could still take Outreau's fine start as the full guarantee—more interesting was the question of the process by which such a history could get itself enacted. The curious thing was that all the while the reasons of her having passed for plain—the reasons for Lady Beldonald's fond calculation, which they quite justified—were written large in her face, so large that it was easy to understand them as the only ones she herself had ever read. What was it then that actually made the old stale sentence mean something so different?—into what new combinations, what extraordinary language, unknown but understood at a glance, had time and life translated it? The only thing to be said was that time and life were artists who beat us all, working with recipes and secrets we could never find out. I really ought to have, like a lecturer or a showman, a chart or a blackboard to present properly the relation, in the wonderful old tender battered blanched face, between the original elements and the exquisite final "style." I could do it with chalks, but I can scarcely do it with words. However, the thing was, for any artist who respected himself, to *feel* it—which I abundantly did;

22

and then not to conceal from *her* I felt it—which I neglected as little. But she was really, to do her complete justice, the last to understand; and I'm not sure that, to the end—for there was an end—she quite made it all out or knew where she was. When you've been brought up for fifty years on black it must be hard to adjust your organism at a day's notice to gold-colour. Her whole nature had been pitched in the key of her supposed plainness. She had known how to be ugly—it was the only thing she had learnt save, if possible, how not to mind it. Being beautiful took in any case a new set of muscles. It was on the prior conviction, literally, that she had developed her admirable dress, instinctively felicitous, always either black or white and a matter of rather severe squareness and studied line. She was magnificently neat; everything she showed had a way of looking both old and fresh; and there was on every occasion the same picture in her draped head—draped in low-falling black—and the fine white plaits (of a painter's white, somehow) disposed on her chest. What had happened was that these arrangements, determined by certain considerations, lent themselves in effect much better to certain others. Adopted in mere shy silence they had really only deepened her accent. It was singular, moreover, that, so constituted, there was nothing in her aspect of the ascetic or the nun. She was a good hard sixteenth-century figure, not withered with innocence, bleached rather by life in the open. She was in short just what we had made of her, a Holbein for a great Museum; and our position, Mrs. Munden's and mine, rapidly became that of persons having such a treasure to dispose of. The world—I speak of course mainly of the art-world—flocked to see it.

CHAPTER IV

"But has she any idea herself, poor thing?" was the way I had put it to Mrs. Munden on our next meeting after the incident at my studio; with the effect, however, only of leaving my friend at first to take me as alluding to Mrs. Brash's possible prevision of the chatter she might create. I had my own sense of that—this provision had been nil; the question was of her consciousness of the office for which Lady Beldonald had counted on her and for which we were so promptly proceeding to spoil her altogether.

"Oh I think she arrived with a goodish notion," Mrs. Munden had replied when I had explained; "for she's clever too, you know, as well as good-looking, and I don't see how, if she ever really *knew* Nina, she could have supposed for a moment that she wasn't wanted for whatever she might have left to give up. Hasn't she moreover always been made to feel that she's ugly enough for anything?" It was even at this point already wonderful how my friend had mastered the case and what lights, alike for its past and its future, she was prepared to throw on it. "If she has seen herself as ugly enough for anything she has seen herself—and that was the only way—as ugly enough for Nina; and she has had her own manner of showing that she understands without making Nina commit herself to anything vulgar. Women are never without ways for doing such things—both for communicating and receiving knowledge—that I can't explain to you, and that you wouldn't understand if I could, since you must be a woman even to do that. I daresay they've expressed it all to each other simply in the language of kisses. But doesn't it at any rate make something rather beautiful of the relation between them as affected by our discovery—?"

I had a laugh for her plural possessive. "The point is of course that if there was a conscious bargain, and our action on Mrs. Brash is to deprive her of the sense of keeping her side of it, various things may happen that won't be good either for her or for ourselves. She may conscientiously throw up the position."

"Yes," my companion mused—"for she is conscientious. Or Nina, without waiting for that, may cast her forth."

I faced it all. "Then we should have to keep her."

"As a regular model?" Mrs. Munden was ready for anything. "Oh that would be lovely!"

But I further worked it out. "The difficulty is that she's not a model, hang it—that she's too good for one, that she's the very thing herself. When Outreau and I have each had our go, that will be all; there'll be nothing left for any one else. Therefore it behoves us quite to understand that our attitude's a responsibility. If we can't do for her positively more than Nina does—"

"We must let her alone?" My companion continued to muse. "I see!"

"Yet don't," I returned, "see too much. We *can* do more."

"Than Nina?" She was again on the spot. "It wouldn't after all be difficult. We only want the directly opposite thing—and which is the only one the poor dear can give. Unless indeed," she suggested, "we simply retract—we back out."

I turned it over. "It's too late for that. Whether Mrs. Brash's peace is gone I can't say. But Nina's is."

"Yes, and there's no way to bring it back that won't sacrifice her friend. We can't turn round and say Mrs. Brash is ugly, can we? But fancy Nina's not having *seen*!" Mrs. Munden exclaimed.

"She doesn't see now," I answered. "She can't, I'm certain, make out what we mean. The woman, for *her* still, is just what she always was. But she has nevertheless had her stroke, and her blindness, while she wavers and gropes in the dark, only adds to her discomfort. Her blow was to see the attention of the world deviate."

"All the same I don't think, you know," my interlocutress said, "that Nina will have made her a scene or that, whatever we do, she'll ever make her one. That isn't the way it will happen, for she's exactly as conscientious as Mrs. Brash."

"Then what is the way?" I asked.

"It will just happen in silence."

"And what will 'it,' as you call it, be?"

"Isn't that what we want really to see?"

"Well," I replied after a turn or two about, "whether we want it or not it's exactly what we *shall* see; which is a reason the more for fancying, between the pair there—in the quiet exquisite house, and full of superiorities and suppressions as they both are—the extraordinary situation. If I said just now that it's too late to do anything but assent it's because I've taken the full measure of what happened at my studio. It took but a few moments—but she tasted of the tree."

My companion wondered. "Nina?"

"Mrs. Brash." And to have to put it so ministered, while I took yet another turn, to a sort of agitation. Our attitude was a responsibility.

But I had suggested something else to my friend, who appeared for a moment detached. "Should you say she'll hate her worse if she *doesn't* see?"

"Lady Beldonald? Doesn't see what we see, you mean, than if she does? Ah I give *that* up!" I laughed. "But what I can tell you is why I hold that, as I said just now, we can do most. We can do this: we can give to a harmless and sensitive creature hitherto practically disinherited—and give with an unexpectedness that will immensely add to its price—the pure joy of a deep draught of the very pride of life, of an acclaimed personal triumph in our superior sophisticated world."

Mrs. Munden had a glow of response for my sudden eloquence. Oh it will be beautiful!

CHAPTER V

Well, that's what, on the whole and in spite of everything, it really was. It has dropped into my memory a rich little gallery of pictures, a regular panorama of those occasions that were to minister to the view from which I had so for a moment extracted a lyric inspiration. I see Mrs. Brash on each of these occasions practically enthroned and surrounded and more or less mobbed; see the hurrying and the nudging and the pressing and the staring; see the people "making up" and introduced, and catch the word when they have had their turn; hear it above all, the great one—"Ah yes, the famous Holbein!"—passed about with that perfection of promptitude that makes the motions of the London mind so happy a mixture of those of the parrot and the sheep. Nothing would be easier of course than to tell the whole little tale with an eye only for that silly side of it. Great was the silliness, but great also as to this case of poor Mrs. Brash, I will say for it, the good nature. Of course, furthermore, it took in particular "our set," with its positive child-terror of the *banal*, to be either so foolish or so wise; though indeed I've never quite known where our set begins and ends, and have had to content myself on this score with the indication once given me by a lady next whom I was placed at dinner: "Oh it's bounded on the north by Ibsen and on the south by Sargent!" Mrs. Brash never sat to me; she absolutely declined; and when she declared that it was quite enough for her that I had with that fine precipitation invited her, I quite took this as she meant it; before we had gone very far our understanding, hers and mine, was complete. Her attitude was as happy as her success was prodigious. The sacrifice of the portrait was a sacrifice to the true inwardness of Lady Beldonald, and did much, for the time, I divined, toward muffling their domestic tension. All it was thus in her power to say—and I heard of a few cases of her having said it—was that she was sure I would have painted her beautifully if she hadn't prevented me. She couldn't even tell the truth, which was that I certainly would have done so if Lady Beldonald hadn't; and she never could mention the subject at all before that personage. I can only describe the affair, naturally, from the outside, and heaven forbid indeed that I should try too closely to, reconstruct the possible strange intercourse of these good friends at home.

My anecdote, however, would lose half the point it may have to show were I to omit all mention of the consummate turn her ladyship appeared gradually to have found herself able to give her deportment. She had made it impossible I should myself bring up our old, our original question, but there was real distinction in her manner of now accepting certain other possibilities. Let me do her that justice; her effort at magnanimity must have been immense. There couldn't fail of course to be ways in which poor Mrs. Brash paid for it. How much she had to pay we were in fact soon enough to see; and it's my intimate conviction that, as a climax, her life at last was the price. But while she lived at least—and it was with an intensity, for those wondrous weeks, of which she had never dreamed—Lady Beldonald herself faced the music. This is what I mean by the possibilities, by the sharp actualities indeed, that she accepted. She took our friend out, she showed her at home, never attempted to hide or to betray her, played her no trick whatever so long as the ordeal lasted. She drank deep, on her side too, of the cup—the cup that for her own lips could only be bitterness. There was, I think, scarce a special success of her companion's at which she wasn't personally present. Mrs. Munden's theory of the silence in which all this would be muffled for them was none the less, and in abundance, confirmed by our observations. The whole thing was to be the death of one or the other of them, but they never spoke of it at tea. I remember even that Nina went so far as to say to me once, looking me full in the eyes, quite sublimely, "I've made out what you mean—she *is* a picture." The beauty of this moreover was that, as I'm persuaded, she hadn't really made it out at all—the words were the mere hypocrisy of her reflective endeavour for virtue. She couldn't possibly have made it out; her friend was as much as ever "dreadfully plain" to her; she must have wondered to the last what on earth possessed us. Wouldn't it in fact have been after all just this failure of vision, this supreme stupidity in short, that kept the catastrophe so long at bay? There was a certain sense of greatness for her in seeing so many of us so absurdly mistaken; and I recall that on various occasions, and in particular when she uttered the words just quoted, this high serenity, as a sign of the relief of her soreness, if not of the effort of her conscience, did

28

something quite visible to my eyes, and also quite unprecedented, for the beauty of her face. She got a real lift from it—such a momentary discernible sublimity that I recollect coming out on the spot with a queer crude amused "Do you know I believe I could paint you *now?*"

She was a fool not to have closed with me then and there; for what has happened since has altered everything—what was to happen a little later was so much more than I could swallow. This was the disappearance of the famous Holbein from one day to the other—producing a consternation among us all as great as if the Venus of Milo had suddenly vanished from the Louvre. "She has simply shipped her straight back"—the explanation was given in that form by Mrs. Munden, who added that any cord pulled tight enough would end at last by snapping. At the snap, in any case, we mightily jumped, for the masterpiece we had for three or four months been living with had made us feel its presence as a luminous lesson and a daily need. We recognised more than ever that it had been, for high finish, the gem of our collection—we found what a blank it left on the wall. Lady Beldonald might fill up the blank, but we couldn't. That she did soon fill it up—and, heaven help us, *how* was put before me after an interval of no great length, but during which I hadn't seen her. I dined on the Christmas of last year at Mrs. Munden's, and Nina, with a "scratch lot," as our hostess said, was there, so that, the preliminary wait being longish, she could approach me very sweetly. "I'll come to you tomorrow if you like," she said; and the effect of it, after a first stare at her, was to make me look all round. I took in, by these two motions, two things; one of which was that, though now again so satisfied herself of her high state, she could give me nothing comparable to what I should have got had she taken me up at the moment of my meeting her on her distinguished concession; the other that she was "suited" afresh and that Mrs. Brash's successor was fully installed. Mrs. Brash's successor, was at the other side of the room, and I became conscious that Mrs. Munden was waiting to see my eyes seek her. I guessed the meaning of the wait; what was one, this time, to say? Oh first and foremost assuredly that it was immensely droll, for this time at least there was no mistake. The lady I looked upon, and as to whom my friend, again quite at sea, appealed to me for a formula, was as little a Holbein, or a specimen of any other school, as she was, like Lady Beldonald herself, a Titian. The

29

formula was easy to give, for the amusement was that her prettiness—yes, literally, prodigiously, her prettiness—was distinct. Lady Beldonald had been magnificent—had been almost intelligent. Miss What's-her-name continues pretty, continues even young, and doesn't matter a straw! She matters so ideally little that Lady Beldonald is practically safer, I judge, than she has ever been. There hasn't been a symptom of chatter about this person, and I believe her protectress is much surprised that we're not more struck.

It was at any rate strictly impossible to me to make an appointment for the day as to which I have just recorded Nina's proposal; and the turn of events since then has not quickened my eagerness. Mrs. Munden remained in correspondence with Mrs. Brash—to the extent, that is, of three letters, each of which she showed me. They so told to our imagination her terrible little story that we were quite prepared—or thought we were—for her going out like a snuffed candle. She resisted, on her return to her original conditions, less than a year; the taste of the tree, as I had called it, had been fatal to her; what she had contentedly enough lived without before for half a century she couldn't now live without for a day. I know nothing of her original conditions—some minor American city—save that for her to have gone back to them was clearly to have stepped out of her frame. We performed, Mrs. Munden and I, a small funeral service for her by talking it all over and making it all out. It wasn't—the minor American city—a market for Holbeins, and what had occurred was that the poor old picture, banished from its museum and refreshed by the rise of no new movement to hang it, was capable of the miracle of a silent revolution; of itself turning, in its dire dishonour, its face to the wall. So it stood, without the intervention of the ghost of a critic, till they happened to pull it round again and find it mere dead paint. Well, it had had, if that's anything, its season of fame, its name on a thousand tongues and printed in capitals in the catalogue. We hadn't been at fault. I haven't, all the same, the least note of her—not a scratch. And I did her so in intention! Mrs. Munden continues to remind me, however, that this is not the sort of rendering with which, on the other side, after all, Lady Beldonald proposes to content herself. She has come back to the question of her own portrait. Let me settle it then at last. Since she *will* have the real thing—well, hang it, she shall!

About Author

Henry James OM (15 April 1843 – 28 February 1916) was an American-British author regarded as a key transitional figure between literary realism and literary modernism, and is considered by many to be among the greatest novelists in the English language. He was the son of Henry James Sr. and the brother of renowned philosopher and psychologist William James and diarist Alice James.

He is best known for a number of novels dealing with the social and marital interplay between émigré Americans, English people, and continental Europeans. Examples of such novels include The Portrait of a Lady, The Ambassadors, and The Wings of the Dove. His later works were increasingly experimental. In describing the internal states of mind and social dynamics of his characters, James often made use of a style in which ambiguous or contradictory motives and impressions were overlaid or juxtaposed in the discussion of a character's psyche. For their unique ambiguity, as well as for other aspects of their composition, his late works have been compared to impressionist painting.

His novella The Turn of the Screw has garnered a reputation as the most analysed and ambiguous ghost story in the English language and remains his most widely adapted work in other media. He also wrote a number of other highly regarded ghost stories and is considered one of the greatest masters of the field.

James published articles and books of criticism, travel, biography, autobiography, and plays. Born in the United States, James largely relocated to Europe as a young man and eventually settled in England, becoming a British subject in 1915, one year before his death. James was nominated for the Nobel Prize in Literature in 1911, 1912 and 1916.

Life

Early years, 1843–1883

James was born at 2 Washington Place in New York City on 15 April 1843. His parents were Mary Walsh and Henry James Sr. His father was intelligent and steadfastly congenial. He was a lecturer and philosopher who had inherited independent means from his father, an Albany banker and investor. Mary came from a wealthy family long settled in New York City. Her sister Katherine lived with her adult family for an extended period of time. Henry Jr. had three brothers, William, who was one year his senior, and younger brothers Wilkinson (Wilkie) and Robertson. His younger sister was Alice. Both of his parents were of Irish and Scottish descent.

The family first lived in Albany, at 70 N. Pearl St., and then moved to Fourteenth Street in New York City when James was still a young boy. His education was calculated by his father to expose him to many influences, primarily scientific and philosophical; it was described by Percy Lubbock, the editor of his selected letters, as "extraordinarily haphazard and promiscuous." James did not share the usual education in Latin and Greek classics. Between 1855 and 1860, the James' household traveled to London, Paris, Geneva, Boulogne-sur-Mer and Newport, Rhode Island, according to the father's current interests and publishing ventures, retreating to the United States when funds were low. Henry studied primarily with tutors and briefly attended schools while the family traveled in Europe. Their longest stays were in France, where Henry began to feel at home and became fluent in French. He was afflicted with a stutter, which seems to have manifested itself only when he spoke English; in French, he did not stutter.

In 1860 the family returned to Newport. There Henry became a friend of the painter John La Farge, who introduced him to French literature, and in particular, to Balzac. James later called Balzac his "greatest master," and said that he had learned more about the craft of fiction from him than from anyone else.

In the autumn of 1861 Henry received an injury, probably to his back, while fighting a fire. This injury, which resurfaced at times throughout his life, made him unfit for military service in the American Civil War.

34

In 1864 the James family moved to Boston, Massachusetts to be near William, who had enrolled first in the Lawrence Scientific School at Harvard and then in the medical school. In 1862 Henry attended Harvard Law School, but realised that he was not interested in studying law. He pursued his interest in literature and associated with authors and critics William Dean Howells and Charles Eliot Norton in Boston and Cambridge, formed lifelong friendships with Oliver Wendell Holmes Jr., the future Supreme Court Justice, and with James and Annie Fields, his first professional mentors.

His first published work was a review of a stage performance, "Miss Maggie Mitchell in Fanchon the Cricket," published in 1863. About a year later, A Tragedy of Error, his first short story, was published anonymously. James's first payment was for an appreciation of Sir Walter Scott's novels, written for the North American Review. He wrote fiction and non-fiction pieces for The Nation and Atlantic Monthly, where Fields was editor. In 1871 he published his first novel, Watch and Ward, in serial form in the Atlantic Monthly. The novel was later published in book form in 1878.

During a 14-month trip through Europe in 1869–70 he met Ruskin, Dickens, Matthew Arnold, William Morris, and George Eliot. Rome impressed him profoundly. "Here I am then in the Eternal City," he wrote to his brother William. "At last—for the first time—I live!" He attempted to support himself as a freelance writer in Rome, then secured a position as Paris correspondent for the New York Tribune, through the influence of its editor John Hay. When these efforts failed he returned to New York City. During 1874 and 1875 he published Transatlantic Sketches, A Passionate Pilgrim, and Roderick Hudson. During this early period in his career he was influenced by Nathaniel Hawthorne.

In 1869 he settled in London. There he established relationships with Macmillan and other publishers, who paid for serial installments that they would later publish in book form. The audience for these serialized novels was largely made up of middle-class women, and James struggled to fashion serious literary work within the strictures imposed by editors' and publishers' notions of what was suitable for young women to read. He lived in rented rooms but was able to join gentlemen's clubs that had libraries and where he could entertain male friends. He was introduced to English society by Henry Adams and Charles Milnes Gaskell, the latter introducing him to the Travellers' and the Reform Clubs.

In the fall of 1875 he moved to the Latin Quarter of Paris. Aside from two trips to America, he spent the next three decades—the rest of his life—in Europe. In Paris he met Zola, Alphonse Daudet, Maupassant, Turgenev, and others. He stayed in Paris only a year before moving to London.

In England he met the leading figures of politics and culture. He continued to be a prolific writer, producing The American (1877), The Europeans (1878), a revision of Watch and Ward (1878), French Poets and Novelists (1878), Hawthorne (1879), and several shorter works of fiction. In 1878 Daisy Miller established his fame on both sides of the Atlantic. It drew notice perhaps mostly because it depicted a woman whose behavior is outside the social norms of Europe. He also began his first masterpiece, The Portrait of a Lady, which would appear in 1881.

In 1877 he first visited Wenlock Abbey in Shropshire, home of his friend Charles Milnes Gaskell whom he had met through Henry Adams. He was much inspired by the darkly romantic Abbey and the surrounding countryside, which features in his essay Abbeys and Castles. In particular the gloomy monastic fishponds behind the Abbey are said to have inspired the lake in The Turn of the Screw.

While living in London, James continued to follow the careers of the "French realists", Émile Zola in particular. Their stylistic methods influenced his own work in the years to come. Hawthorne's influence on him faded during this period, replaced by George Eliot and Ivan Turgenev. 1879–1882 saw the publication of The Europeans, Washington Square, Confidence, and The Portrait of a Lady. He visited America in 1882–1883, then returned to London.

The period from 1881 to 1883 was marked by several losses. His mother died in 1881, followed by his father a few months later, and then by his brother Wilkie. Emerson, an old family friend, died in 1882. His friend Turgenev died in 1883.

Middle years, 1884–1897

In 1884 James made another visit to Paris. There he met again with Zola, Daudet, and Goncourt. He had been following the careers of the French "realist" or "naturalist" writers, and was increasingly influenced by them. In 1886, he published The Bostonians and The Princess Casamassima, both influenced by the French writers he'd studied assiduously. Critical reaction and sales were poor. He wrote to Howells that the books had hurt his career rather than helped because they had "reduced the desire, and demand, for my productions to zero". During this time he became friends with Robert Louis Stevenson, John Singer Sargent, Edmund Gosse, George du Maurier, Paul Bourget, and Constance Fenimore Woolson. His third novel from the 1880s was The Tragic Muse. Although he was following the precepts of Zola in his novels of the '80s, their tone and attitude are closer to the fiction of Alphonse Daudet. The lack of critical and financial success for his novels during this period led him to try writing for the theatre. (His dramatic works and his experiences with theatre are discussed below.)

In the last quarter of 1889, he started translating "for pure and copious lucre" Port Tarascon, the third volume of Alphonse Daudet adventures of Tartarin de Tarascon. Serialized in Harper's Monthly Magazine from June 1890, this translation praised as "clever" by The Spectator was published in January 1891 by Sampson Low, Marston, Searle & Rivington.

After the stage failure of Guy Domville in 1895, James was near despair and thoughts of death plagued him. The years spent on dramatic works were not entirely a loss. As he moved into the last phase of his career he found ways to adapt dramatic techniques into the novel form.

In the late 1880s and throughout the 1890s James made several trips through Europe. He spent a long stay in Italy in 1887. In that year the short novel The Aspern Papers and The Reverberator were published.

Late years, 1898–1916

In 1897–1898 he moved to Rye, Sussex, and wrote The Turn of the Screw. 1899–1900 saw the publication of The Awkward Age and The Sacred

Fount. During 1902–1904 he wrote The Ambassadors, The Wings of the Dove, and The Golden Bowl.

In 1904 he revisited America and lectured on Balzac. In 1906–1910 he published The American Scene and edited the "New York Edition", a 24-volume collection of his works. In 1910 his brother William died; Henry had just joined William from an unsuccessful search for relief in Europe on what then turned out to be his (Henry's) last visit to the United States (from summer 1910 to July 1911), and was near him, according to a letter he wrote, when he died.

In 1913 he wrote his autobiographies, A Small Boy and Others, and Notes of a Son and Brother. After the outbreak of the First World War in 1914 he did war work. In 1915 he became a British subject and was awarded the Order of Merit the following year. He died on 28 February 1916, in Chelsea, London. As he requested, his ashes were buried in Cambridge Cemetery in Massachusetts.

Biographers

James regularly rejected suggestions that he should marry, and after settling in London proclaimed himself "a bachelor". F. W. Dupee, in several volumes on the James family, originated the theory that he had been in love with his cousin Mary ("Minnie") Temple, but that a neurotic fear of sex kept him from admitting such affections: "James's invalidism ... was itself the symptom of some fear of or scruple against sexual love on his part." Dupee used an episode from James's memoir A Small Boy and Others, recounting a dream of a Napoleonic image in the Louvre, to exemplify James's romanticism about Europe, a Napoleonic fantasy into which he fled.

Dupee had not had access to the James family papers and worked principally from James's published memoir of his older brother, William, and the limited collection of letters edited by Percy Lubbock, heavily weighted toward James's last years. His account therefore moved directly from James's childhood, when he trailed after his older brother, to elderly invalidism. As more material became available to scholars, including the diaries of contemporaries and hundreds of affectionate and sometimes erotic letters written by James to younger men, the picture of neurotic celibacy gave way to a portrait of a closeted homosexual.

Between 1953 and 1972, Leon Edel authored a major five-volume biography of James, which accessed unpublished letters and documents after Edel gained the permission of James's family. Edel's portrayal of James included the suggestion he was celibate. It was a view first propounded by critic Saul Rosenzweig in 1943. In 1996 Sheldon M. Novick published Henry James: The Young Master, followed by Henry James: The Mature Master (2007). The first book "caused something of an uproar in Jamesian circles" as it challenged the previous received notion of celibacy, a once-familiar paradigm in biographies of homosexuals when direct evidence was non-existent. Novick also criticised Edel for following the discounted Freudian interpretation of homosexuality "as a kind of failure." The difference of opinion erupted in a series of exchanges between Edel and Novick which were published by the online magazine Slate, with the latter arguing that even the suggestion of celibacy went against James's own injunction "live!"—not "fantasize!"

A letter James wrote in old age to Hugh Walpole has been cited as an explicit statement of this. Walpole confessed to him of indulging in "high jinks", and James wrote a reply endorsing it: "We must know, as much as possible, in our beautiful art, yours & mine, what we are talking about — & the only way to know it is to have lived & loved & cursed & floundered & enjoyed & suffered — I don't think I regret a single 'excess' of my responsive youth".

The interpretation of James as living a less austere emotional life has been subsequently explored by other scholars. The often intense politics of Jamesian scholarship has also been the subject of studies. Author Colm Tóibín has said that Eve Kosofsky Sedgwick's Epistemology of the Closet made a landmark difference to Jamesian scholarship by arguing that he be read as a homosexual writer whose desire to keep his sexuality a secret shaped his layered style and dramatic artistry. According to Tóibín such a reading "removed James from the realm of dead white males who wrote about posh people. He became our contemporary."

James's letters to expatriate American sculptor Hendrik Christian Andersen have attracted particular attention. James met the 27-year-old Andersen in Rome in 1899, when James was 56, and wrote letters to Andersen that are intensely emotional: "I hold you, dearest boy, in my innermost love, & count on your feeling me—in every throb of your soul". In a letter of 6 May 1904, to his brother William, James referred to himself as "always your hopelessly celibate even though sexagenarian Henry". How accurate that description might have been is the subject of contention among James's biographers, but the letters to Andersen were occasionally quasi-erotic: "I put, my dear boy, my arm around you, & feel the pulsation, thereby, as it were, of our excellent future & your admirable endowment." To his homosexual friend Howard Sturgis, James could write: "I repeat, almost to indiscretion, that I could live with you. Meanwhile I can only try to live without you."

His numerous letters to the many young gay men among his close male friends are more forthcoming. In a letter to Howard Sturgis, following a long visit, James refers jocularly to their "happy little congress of two" and in letters to Hugh Walpole he pursues convoluted jokes and puns about their relationship, referring to himself as an elephant who "paws you oh so benevolently" and winds about Walpole his "well meaning old trunk". His letters to Walter Berry printed by the Black Sun Press have long been celebrated for their lightly veiled eroticism.

He corresponded in almost equally extravagant language with his many female friends, writing, for example, to fellow novelist Lucy Clifford: "Dearest Lucy! What shall I say? when I love you so very, very much, and see you nine times for once that I see Others! Therefore I think that—if you want it made clear to the meanest intelligence—I love you more than I love Others." To his New York friend Mary Cadwalader Jones: "Dearest Mary Cadwalader. I yearn over you, but I yearn in vain; & your long silence really breaks my heart, mystifies, depresses, almost alarms me, to the point even of making me wonder if poor unconscious & doting old Célimare [Jones's pet name for James] has 'done' anything, in some dark somnambulism of the spirit, which has ... given you a bad moment, or a wrong impression, or a 'colourable pretext' ... However these things may be, he loves you as tenderly as ever;

nothing, to the end of time, will ever detach him from you, & he remembers those Eleventh St. matutinal intimes hours, those telephonic matinées, as the most romantic of his life ..." His long friendship with American novelist Constance Fenimore Woolson, in whose house he lived for a number of weeks in Italy in 1887, and his shock and grief over her suicide in 1894, are discussed in detail in Edel's biography and play a central role in a study by Lyndall Gordon. (Edel conjectured that Woolson was in love with James and killed herself in part because of his coldness, but Woolson's biographers have objected to Edel's account.)

Works

Style and themes

James is one of the major figures of trans-Atlantic literature. His works frequently juxtapose characters from the Old World (Europe), embodying a feudal civilisation that is beautiful, often corrupt, and alluring, and from the New World (United States), where people are often brash, open, and assertive and embody the virtues—freedom and a more highly evolved moral character—of the new American society. James explores this clash of personalities and cultures, in stories of personal relationships in which power is exercised well or badly. His protagonists were often young American women facing oppression or abuse, and as his secretary Theodora Bosanquet remarked in her monograph Henry James at Work:

> When he walked out of the refuge of his study and into the world and looked around him, he saw a place of torment, where creatures of prey perpetually thrust their claws into the quivering flesh of doomed, defenseless children of light ... His novels are a repeated exposure of this wickedness, a reiterated and passionate plea for the fullest freedom of development, unimperiled by reckless and barbarous stupidity.

Critics have jokingly described three phases in the development of James's prose: "James I, James II, and The Old Pretender." He wrote short stories and plays. Finally, in his third and last period he returned to the long, serialised novel. Beginning in the second period, but most noticeably in the third, he increasingly abandoned direct statement in favour of frequent

41

double negatives, and complex descriptive imagery. Single paragraphs began to run for page after page, in which an initial noun would be succeeded by pronouns surrounded by clouds of adjectives and prepositional clauses, far from their original referents, and verbs would be deferred and then preceded by a series of adverbs. The overall effect could be a vivid evocation of a scene as perceived by a sensitive observer. It has been debated whether this change of style was engendered by James's shifting from writing to dictating to a typist, a change made during the composition of What Maisie Knew.

In its intense focus on the consciousness of his major characters, James's later work foreshadows extensive developments in 20th century fiction. Indeed, he might have influenced stream-of-consciousness writers such as Virginia Woolf, who not only read some of his novels but also wrote essays about them. Both contemporary and modern readers have found the late style difficult and unnecessary; his friend Edith Wharton, who admired him greatly, said that there were passages in his work that were all but incomprehensible. James was harshly portrayed by H. G. Wells as a hippopotamus laboriously attempting to pick up a pea that had got into a corner of its cage. The "late James" style was ably parodied by Max Beerbohm in "The Mote in the Middle Distance".

More important for his work overall may have been his position as an expatriate, and in other ways an outsider, living in Europe. While he came from middle-class and provincial beginnings (seen from the perspective of European polite society) he worked very hard to gain access to all levels of society, and the settings of his fiction range from working class to aristocratic, and often describe the efforts of middle-class Americans to make their way in European capitals. He confessed he got some of his best story ideas from gossip at the dinner table or at country house weekends. He worked for a living, however, and lacked the experiences of select schools, university, and army service, the common bonds of masculine society. He was furthermore a man whose tastes and interests were, according to the prevailing standards of Victorian era Anglo-American culture, rather feminine, and who was shadowed by the cloud of prejudice that then and later accompanied suspicions of his homosexuality. Edmund Wilson famously compared James's objectivity to Shakespeare's:

One would be in a position to appreciate James better if one compared him with the dramatists of the seventeenth century—Racine and Molière, whom he resembles in form as well as in point of view, and even Shakespeare, when allowances are made for the most extreme differences in subject and form. These poets are not, like Dickens and Hardy, writers of melodrama—either humorous or pessimistic, nor secretaries of society like Balzac, nor prophets like Tolstoy: they are occupied simply with the presentation of conflicts of moral character, which they do not concern themselves about softening or averting. They do not indict society for these situations: they regard them as universal and inevitable. They do not even blame God for allowing them: they accept them as the conditions of life.

It is also possible to see many of James's stories as psychological thought-experiments. In his preface to the New York edition of The American he describes the development of the story in his mind as exactly such: the "situation" of an American, "some robust but insidiously beguiled and betrayed, some cruelly wronged, compatriot..." with the focus of the story being on the response of this wronged man. The Portrait of a Lady may be an experiment to see what happens when an idealistic young woman suddenly becomes very rich. In many of his tales, characters seem to exemplify alternative futures and possibilities, as most markedly in "The Jolly Corner", in which the protagonist and a ghost-doppelganger live alternative American and European lives; and in others, like The Ambassadors, an older James seems fondly to regard his own younger self facing a crucial moment.

Major novels

The first period of James's fiction, usually considered to have culminated in The Portrait of a Lady, concentrated on the contrast between Europe and America. The style of these novels is generally straightforward and, though personally characteristic, well within the norms of 19th-century fiction. Roderick Hudson (1875) is a Künstlerroman that traces the development of the title character, an extremely talented sculptor. Although the book shows some signs of immaturity—this was James's first serious attempt at a full-length novel—it has attracted favourable comment due to the vivid realisation of the three major characters: Roderick Hudson, superbly gifted but unstable and unreliable; Rowland Mallet, Roderick's limited but much more mature friend and patron; and Christina Light, one of James's most enchanting and maddening femmes fatales. The pair of Hudson and Mallet has been seen as representing the two sides of James's own nature: the wildly imaginative artist and the brooding conscientious mentor.

In The Portrait of a Lady (1881) James concluded the first phase of his career with a novel that remains his most popular piece of long fiction. The story is of a spirited young American woman, Isabel Archer, who "affronts her destiny" and finds it overwhelming. She inherits a large amount of money and subsequently becomes the victim of Machiavellian scheming by two American expatriates. The narrative is set mainly in Europe, especially in England and Italy. Generally regarded as the masterpiece of his early phase, The Portrait of a Lady is described as a psychological novel, exploring the minds of his characters, and almost a work of social science, exploring the differences between Europeans and Americans, the old and the new worlds.

The second period of James's career, which extends from the publication of The Portrait of a Lady through the end of the nineteenth century, features less popular novels including The Princess Casamassima, published serially in The Atlantic Monthly in 1885–1886, and The Bostonians, published serially in The Century Magazine during the same period. This period also featured James's celebrated Gothic novella, The Turn of the Screw.

The third period of James's career reached its most significant achievement in three novels published just around the start of the 20th century: The Wings of the Dove (1902), The Ambassadors (1903), and The Golden Bowl (1904). Critic F. O. Matthiessen called this "trilogy" James's major phase, and these novels have certainly received intense critical study. It was the second-written of the books, The Wings of the Dove (1902) that was the first published because it attracted no serialization. This novel tells the story of Milly Theale, an American heiress stricken with a serious disease, and her impact on the people around her. Some of these people befriend Milly with honourable motives, while others are more self-interested. James stated in his autobiographical books that Milly was based on Minny Temple, his beloved cousin who died at an early age of tuberculosis. He said that he attempted in the novel to wrap her memory in the "beauty and dignity of art".

Shorter narratives

James was particularly interested in what he called the "beautiful and blest nouvelle", or the longer form of short narrative. Still, he produced a number of very short stories in which he achieved notable compression of sometimes complex subjects. The following narratives are representative of James's achievement in the shorter forms of fiction.

- "A Tragedy of Error" (1864), short story

- "The Story of a Year" (1865), short story

- A Passionate Pilgrim (1871), novella

- Madame de Mauves (1874), novella

- Daisy Miller (1878), novella

- The Aspern Papers (1888), novella

- The Lesson of the Master (1888), novella

- The Pupil (1891), short story

- "The Figure in the Carpet" (1896), short story

- The Beast in the Jungle (1903), novella

- An International Episode (1878)

- Picture and Text

- Four Meetings (1885)

- A London Life, and Other Tales (1889)

- The Spoils of Poynton (1896)

- Embarrassments (1896)

- The Two Magics: The Turn of the Screw, Covering End (1898)

- A Little Tour of France (1900)

- The Sacred Fount (1901)

- Views and Reviews (1908)

- The Wings of the Dove, Volume I (1902)

- The Wings of the Dove, Volume II (1909)

- The Finer Grain (1910)

- The Outcry (1911)

- Lady Barbarina: The Siege of London, An International Episode and Other Tales (1922)

- The Birthplace (1922)

Plays

At several points in his career James wrote plays, beginning with one-act plays written for periodicals in 1869 and 1871 and a dramatisation of his popular novella Daisy Miller in 1882. From 1890 to 1892, having received a bequest that freed him from magazine publication, he made a strenuous effort to succeed on the London stage, writing a half-dozen plays of which only one, a dramatisation of his novel The American, was produced. This play was performed for several years by a touring repertory company and had a respectable run in London, but did not earn very much money for James. His other plays written at this time were not produced.

In 1893, however, he responded to a request from actor-manager George Alexander for a serious play for the opening of his renovated St. James's Theatre, and wrote a long drama, Guy Domville, which Alexander produced. There was a noisy uproar on the opening night, 5 January 1895, with hissing from the gallery when James took his bow after the final curtain, and the author was upset. The play received moderately good reviews and had a modest run of four weeks before being taken off to make way for Oscar Wilde's The Importance of Being Earnest, which Alexander thought would have better prospects for the coming season.

After the stresses and disappointment of these efforts James insisted that he would write no more for the theatre, but within weeks had agreed to write a curtain-raiser for Ellen Terry. This became the one-act "Summersoft", which he later rewrote into a short story, "Covering End", and then expanded into a full-length play, The High Bid, which had a brief run in London in 1907, when James made another concerted effort to write for the stage. He wrote three new plays, two of which were in production when the death of Edward VII on 6 May 1910 plunged London into mourning and theatres closed. Discouraged by failing health and the stresses of theatrical work, James did not renew his efforts in the theatre, but recycled his plays as successful novels. The Outcry was a best-seller in the United States when it was published in 1911. During the years 1890–1893 when he was most engaged with the theatre, James wrote a good deal of theatrical criticism and assisted Elizabeth Robins and others in translating and producing Henrik Ibsen for the first time in London.

Leon Edel argued in his psychoanalytic biography that James was traumatised by the opening night uproar that greeted Guy Domville, and that it plunged him into a prolonged depression. The successful later novels, in Edel's view, were the result of a kind of self-analysis, expressed in fiction, which partly freed him from his fears. Other biographers and scholars have not accepted this account, however; the more common view being that of F.O. Matthiessen, who wrote: "Instead of being crushed by the collapse of his hopes [for the theatre]... he felt a resurgence of new energy."

Non-fiction

Beyond his fiction, James was one of the more important literary critics in the history of the novel. In his classic essay The Art of Fiction (1884), he argued against rigid prescriptions on the novelist's choice of subject and method of treatment. He maintained that the widest possible freedom in content and approach would help ensure narrative fiction's continued vitality.

James wrote many valuable critical articles on other novelists; typical is his book-length study of Nathaniel Hawthorne, which has been the subject of critical debate. Richard Brodhead has suggested that the study was emblematic of James's struggle with Hawthorne's influence, and constituted an effort to place the elder writer "at a disadvantage." Gordon Fraser, meanwhile, has suggested that the study was part of a more commercial effort by James to introduce himself to British readers as Hawthorne's natural successor.

When James assembled the New York Edition of his fiction in his final years, he wrote a series of prefaces that subjected his own work to searching, occasionally harsh criticism.

At 22 James wrote The Noble School of Fiction for The Nation's first issue in 1865. He would write, in all, over 200 essays and book, art, and theatre reviews for the magazine.

For most of his life James harboured ambitions for success as a playwright. He converted his novel The American into a play that enjoyed modest returns in the early 1890s. In all he wrote about a dozen plays, most of which went unproduced. His costume drama Guy Domville failed disastrously on its opening night in 1895. James then largely abandoned his efforts to conquer the stage and returned to his fiction. In his Notebooks he maintained that his theatrical experiment benefited his novels and tales by helping him dramatise his characters' thoughts and emotions. James produced a small but valuable amount of theatrical criticism, including perceptive appreciations of Henrik Ibsen.

With his wide-ranging artistic interests, James occasionally wrote on the visual arts. Perhaps his most valuable contribution was his favourable assessment of fellow expatriate John Singer Sargent, a painter whose critical status has improved markedly in recent decades. James also wrote sometimes charming, sometimes brooding articles about various places he visited and lived in. His most famous books of travel writing include Italian Hours (an example of the charming approach) and The American Scene (most definitely on the brooding side).

James was one of the great letter-writers of any era. More than ten thousand of his personal letters are extant, and over three thousand have been published in a large number of collections. A complete edition of James's letters began publication in 2006, edited by Pierre Walker and Greg Zacharias. As of 2014, eight volumes have been published, covering the period from 1855 to 1880. James's correspondents included celebrated contemporaries like Robert Louis Stevenson, Edith Wharton and Joseph Conrad, along with many others in his wide circle of friends and acquaintances. The letters range from the "mere twaddle of graciousness" to serious discussions of artistic, social and personal issues.

Very late in life James began a series of autobiographical works: A Small Boy and Others, Notes of a Son and Brother, and the unfinished The Middle Years. These books portray the development of a classic observer who was passionately interested in artistic creation but was somewhat reticent about participating fully in the life around him.

Reception

Criticism, biographies and fictional treatments

James's work has remained steadily popular with the limited audience of educated readers to whom he spoke during his lifetime, and has remained firmly in the canon, but, after his death, some American critics, such as Van Wyck Brooks, expressed hostility towards James for his long expatriation and eventual naturalisation as a British subject. Other critics such as E. M. Forster complained about what they saw as James's squeamishness in the treatment of sex and other possibly controversial material, or dismissed his late style as difficult and obscure, relying heavily on extremely long sentences and excessively latinate language. Similarly Oscar Wilde criticised him for writing "fiction as if it were a painful duty". Vernon Parrington, composing a canon of American literature, condemned James for having cut himself off from America. Jorge Luis Borges wrote about him, "Despite the scruples and delicate complexities of James, his work suffers from a major defect: the absence of life." And Virginia Woolf, writing to Lytton Strachey, asked, "Please tell me what you find in Henry James. ... we have his works here, and

I read, and I can't find anything but faintly tinged rose water, urbane and sleek, but vulgar and pale as Walter Lamb. Is there really any sense in it?" The novelist W. Somerset Maugham wrote, "He did not know the English as an Englishman instinctively knows them and so his English characters never to my mind quite ring true," and argued "The great novelists, even in seclusion, have lived life passionately. Henry James was content to observe it from a window." Maugham nevertheless wrote, "The fact remains that those last novels of his, notwithstanding their unreality, make all other novels, except the very best, unreadable." Colm Tóibín observed that James "never really wrote about the English very well. His English characters don't work for me."

Despite these criticisms, James is now valued for his psychological and moral realism, his masterful creation of character, his low-key but playful humour, and his assured command of the language. In his 1983 book, The Novels of Henry James, Edward Wagenknecht offers an assessment that echoes Theodora Bosanquet's:

> "To be completely great," Henry James wrote in an early review, "a work of art must lift up the heart," and his own novels do this to an outstanding degree ... More than sixty years after his death, the great novelist who sometimes professed to have no opinions stands foursquare in the great Christian humanistic and democratic tradition. The men and women who, at the height of World War II, raided the secondhand shops for his out-of-print books knew what they were about. For no writer ever raised a braver banner to which all who love freedom might adhere.

William Dean Howells saw James as a representative of a new realist school of literary art which broke with the English romantic tradition epitomised by the works of Charles Dickens and William Makepeace Thackeray. Howells wrote that realism found "its chief exemplar in Mr. James... A novelist he is not, after the old fashion, or after any fashion but his own." F.R. Leavis championed Henry James as a novelist of "established pre-eminence" in The Great Tradition (1948), asserting that The Portrait of a Lady and The Bostonians were "the two most brilliant novels in the language." James is now prized as a master of point of view who moved literary fiction forward by insisting in showing, not telling, his stories to the reader. (Source: Wikipedia)

NOTABLE WORKS

NOVELS

Watch and Ward (1871)

Roderick Hudson (1875)

The American (1877)

The Europeans (1878)

Confidence (1879)

Washington Square (1880)

The Portrait of a Lady (1881)

The Bostonians (1886)

The Princess Casamassima (1886)

The Reverberator (1888)

The Tragic Muse (1890)

The Other House (1896)

The Spoils of Poynton (1897)

What Maisie Knew (1897)

The Awkward Age (1899)

The Sacred Fount (1901)

The Wings of the Dove (1902)

The Ambassadors (1903)

The Golden Bowl (1904)

The Whole Family (collaborative novel with eleven other authors, 1908)

The Outcry (1911)

The Ivory Tower (unfinished, published posthumously 1917)

The Sense of the Past (unfinished, published posthumously 1917)

SHORT STORIES AND NOVELLAS

A Tragedy of Error (1864)

The Story of a Year (1865)

A Landscape Painter (1866)

A Day of Days (1866)

My Friend Bingham (1867)

Poor Richard (1867)

The Story of a Masterpiece (1868)

A Most Extraordinary Case (1868)

A Problem (1868)

De Grey: A Romance (1868)

Osborne's Revenge (1868)

The Romance of Certain Old Clothes (1868)

A Light Man (1869)

Gabrielle de Bergerac (1869)

Travelling Companions (1870)

A Passionate Pilgrim (1871)

At Isella (1871)

Master Eustace (1871)

Guest's Confession (1872)

The Madonna of the Future (1873)

The Sweetheart of M. Briseux (1873)

The Last of the Valerii (1874)

Madame de Mauves (1874)

Adina (1874)

Professor Fargo (1874)

Eugene Pickering (1874)

Benvolio (1875)

Crawford's Consistency (1876)

The Ghostly Rental (1876)

Four Meetings (1877)

Rose-Agathe (1878, as Théodolinde)

Daisy Miller (1878)

Longstaff's Marriage (1878)

An International Episode (1878)

The Pension Beaurepas (1879)

A Diary of a Man of Fifty (1879)

A Bundle of Letters (1879)

The Point of View (1882)

The Siege of London (1883)

Impressions of a Cousin (1883)

Lady Barberina (1884)

Pandora (1884)

The Author of Beltraffio (1884)

Georgina's Reasons (1884)

A New England Winter (1884)

The Path of Duty (1884)

Mrs. Temperly (1887)

Louisa Pallant (1888)

The Aspern Papers (1888)

The Liar (1888)

The Modern Warning (1888, originally published as The Two Countries)

A London Life (1888)

The Patagonia (1888)

The Lesson of the Master (1888)

The Solution (1888)

The Pupil (1891)

Brooksmith (1891)

The Marriages (1891)

The Chaperon (1891)

Sir Edmund Orme (1891)

Nona Vincent (1892)

The Real Thing (1892)

The Private Life (1892)

Lord Beaupré (1892)

The Visits (1892)

Sir Dominick Ferrand (1892)

Greville Fane (1892)

Collaboration (1892)

Owen Wingrave (1892)

The Wheel of Time (1892)

The Middle Years (1893)

The Death of the Lion (1894)

The Coxon Fund (1894)

The Next Time (1895)

Glasses (1896)

The Altar of the Dead (1895)

The Figure in the Carpet (1896)

The Way It Came (1896, also published as The Friends of the Friends)

The Turn of the Screw (1898)

Covering End (1898)

In the Cage (1898)

John Delavoy (1898)

The Given Case (1898)

Europe (1899)

The Great Condition (1899)

The Real Right Thing (1899)

Paste (1899)

The Great Good Place (1900)

Maud-Evelyn (1900)

Miss Gunton of Poughkeepsie (1900)

The Tree of Knowledge (1900)

The Abasement of the Northmores (1900)

The Third Person (1900)

The Special Type (1900)

The Tone of Time (1900)

Broken Wings (1900)

The Two Faces (1900)

Mrs. Medwin (1901)

The Beldonald Holbein (1901)

The Story in It (1902)

Flickerbridge (1902)

The Birthplace (1903)

The Beast in the Jungle (1903)

The Papers (1903)

Fordham Castle (1904)

Julia Bride (1908)

The Jolly Corner (1908)

The Velvet Glove (1909)

Mora Montravers (1909)

Crapy Cornelia (1909)

The Bench of Desolation (1909)

A Round of Visits (1910)

OTHER

Transatlantic Sketches (1875)

French Poets and Novelists (1878)

Hawthorne (1879)

Portraits of Places (1883)

A Little Tour in France (1884)

Partial Portraits (1888)

Essays in London and Elsewhere (1893)

Picture and Text (1893)

Terminations (1893)

Theatricals (1894)

Theatricals: Second Series (1895)

Guy Domville (1895)

The Soft Side (1900)

William Wetmore Story and His Friends (1903)

The Better Sort (1903)

English Hours (1905)

The Question of our Speech; The Lesson of Balzac. Two Lectures (1905)

The American Scene (1907)

Views and Reviews (1908)

Italian Hours (1909)

A Small Boy and Others (1913)

Notes on Novelists (1914)

Notes of a Son and Brother (1914)

Within the Rim (1918)

Travelling Companions (1919)

Notebooks (various, published posthumously)

The Middle Years (unfinished, published posthumously 1917)

A Most Unholy Trade (1925, published posthumously)

The Art of the Novel : Critical Prefaces (1934)

CPSIA information can be obtained
at www.ICGtesting.com
Printed in the USA
LVHW091914191020
669187LV00003B/11

9 781662 718977